STRUNG OUT ON PLENITUDES

Bobby Goldner

First published by Disarticulated Press 2025

Thank you to the people who helped me along the way.
Greig Thomson, L.O.G., R.M. Greta, Sapna, S.M., Valerie Wade

First edition

ISBN: 978-1-76-420194-0

Editing by Greig Thomson

For my father

I

Part One

Uzis and Lean and all of the Wars in Between

1

Eastern Grooming, Salamanders and Geopolitics

I remember her first fainting incident; we were both very nonchalant about it. It was around two o'clock in the morning, and I woke up from a nightmare. I wasn't quite startled, and I'm not really sure if it was a nightmare or just an abstract dream. I couldn't always distinguish between the two.

Something about the abstract in the waking world appealed to me, but not so much in dreams. I always wanted to see a Rothko in person, but it never happened. I was, however, conceived when my parents visited Washington, D.C. in the summer of '75 to see the inaugural exhibition at the Hirshhorn Museum and Sculpture Garden at the Smithsonian. My mother once told me that besides conceiving me, seeing the Rothko paintings on that trip was the highlight.

I could handle a nightmare. But seeing Grover from Sesame Street—specifically *Super Grover*, red cape and all—staring at me for hours while screaming in a high-pitched sine wave tone? That was something I couldn't handle. It wasn't quite a nightmare, but the scene was blurry enough to be a Color Field painting much like Rothko's.

About thirty minutes later, Naomi woke up to my tossing and turning.

"Another nightmare?"

"I'm not sure that it was a nightmare," I replied.

"Oh so we're Abstract Expressionists tonight?"

I gave her a grunt and a smirk. She got up to pee, and that was how the first fainting incident occurred. It wasn't dramatic. She was anemic, and her doctor did warn her about orthostatic hypotension. She simply must have gotten out of bed too quickly, we thought. And now we sit here at the oncologist's office, waiting for her to be seen by Dr. Reece.

* * *

My phone was dying. It felt like my phone was always dying these days. I ruffled through the magazine stack and came across a yellow journal titled *Strung Out on Plenitudes*. It was a book of hand-written quotes. Attributions and all. The first read:

> Thank you, I appreciate the compliment. I carefully shave the hair on my mons pubis into a perfect equilateral triangle, as in some Asian cultures triangles are seen as symbols of good fortune. It is my Pascal's triangle inverted, a visual representation of binomial coefficients, a perfect form for luck. The higher inverted triangle has its vertices placed at the

> southern tip of my pubis, my western nipple, and my eastern nipple. This is my Sierpiński triangle, a lucky self-similar fractal that is equilateral like my lower Pascal's triangle. My anus is left unwaxed, a simple enso, commonly known as a Zen circle, representing enlightenment. Its imperfection signifies the Japanese aesthetic of wabi-sabi, and I leave the hairs in a state of impermanence rising from the natural cycle of growth and decay. This is why I only participate in transient butt sex.

Margaret Thatcher to her gynecologist, 1988

Naomi asked what I was laughing at. I didn't quite know how to answer without showing her the journal, but I didn't have to.

"Naomi Malone? The doctor is ready to see you."

I asked, "Want me to come in with you this time?"

"No," she said. "She's probably going to give me blood or run some tests. Who knows anymore? I might be in there for a while."

I glanced back down at the yellow journal and smirked. It felt like I was always smirking these days.

* * *

A slender mother and a young girl gracefully entered the waiting room. Graceful as if they knew every strand of the gray matted carpet that they strode across. The young girl was completely hairless, from head to eyebrows. She was all of St. Jude Children's Research Hospital in pajamas. The pajamas were pastel blue, with little pink lizards on them. Axolotls I think they are called.

The young girl looked at me and smiled a cancer smile as they were waiting at the front desk to be checked in. I huffed my cheeks up like an Indian Yellow Bullfrog and swiftly collapsed them with my palms, letting out a quiet farting sound. She giggled and then let her gaze wander back to the front desk, as if the quiet farting sound incident never happened. It's probably a cancer thing, I thought, the lack of prolonged eye contact.

I fiddled with my phone for a minute to check my emails, but it quickly died. I returned to the yellow journal. What a story that was. Thatcher and all! I continued reading.

> Axolotls, the paedomorphic salamanders, are all the rage these days. Children even have axolotl plushies, despite the cute little guys being critically endangered with an estimated 50 to 1,000 axolotls remaining in their natural habitat in the Xochimilco canals of Mexico City. Now they are relegated to captivity in tanks across the world. We are preserving a species because they are, well, they are cute. But what of the critically endangered Chinese giant salamander? Nobody cares because they are fat and ugly, kind of like you my dear. Or maybe it's because they are from China. Is Mexico more popular than China now? I can't keep up with geopolitics these days. Now ugly fat men, like you my dear, I understand. You prefer fistfuls of dumplings over tamales. You eat so many dumplings,

> you are going to turn into a fat and ugly Chinese giant salamander. Maybe try a salad tonight dear. It'll be a turn on for me. We'll make love, and I'll try to bear the weight of you climbing on top of me, all out of breath with slimy sweaty skin like a naked-toed gecko.

Elizabeth Shatner to her husband, William Shatner, 2020

Huh. Axolotls, I thought. What a bizarre coincidence. Then a Pedego Electric Bikes commercial came on the waiting room television, delivered by non other than William Shatner. Slimy sweaty skin and all. I did not smirk.

2

Rachel's Curiosity, Pandiculation, At the Dog Park

You see, extreme coincidences were not novel for me. I had a psychotic break in 2017, centered around delusions of grandeur and synchronicity. I saw patterns in everything, and coincidences abounded. I felt that a shamanic form of wisdom had come to me. And I sure was vocal about it too. I was institutionalized for a week and administered all kinds of pills. Lithium, risperidone, clonazepam, and four others I can't remember. The magical life of a shaman noodling parts of the universe into synchronous orbits disappeared after a few weeks. I don't like to think about it. Especially my time in the institution.

In subsequent therapy, part of my recovery was confronting this synchronicity head on and not let it fester inside of me. My psychiatrist told me it was possible that I had a type of neurodivergent pattern recognition, commonly seen in the autistic. She never told me if I was autistic though. It wouldn't have fazed me. I had a mildly autistic friend in college. He was a great fellow.

I think his name was Tony, but we called him Fucko. He was one of those lumbering super wide-trunked type of guys with wild curly blonde hair who played lacrosse. I didn't even know my college had a lacrosse team until I met him. For all I knew, he *was* the lacrosse team. He stole cases of beer from the frat parties we weren't welcome at. He did this with no pretense of a thief. No shady antics and no scheming. He would just walk into the Kappa Alpha whatever-the-fuck house and grab a case. I mean, who was going to stop Fucko?

My thoughts of the mildly autistic Fucko faded into the ceiling's fluorescent bulbs. I glanced at the yellow journal on my lap and realized that putting it aside would be contrary to the lessons I learned in therapy. I was not a mystic. I was just a little different. Maybe a bit like Fucko.

Confront this synchronicity head on. Do not let it fester inside of you.

So I flipped the page.

> I must have been around seven. I wondered what was so special about the bag my mother held to her chest that Monday evening. Was it a bag full of roses? Were we going to visit grandmother at the cemetery? The way she protected the bag, holding it close to her heart, meant it was surely something to be adored. I remember tugging on the bottom until it tore. Pill bottle after pill bottle spilled out like I had just broke open a sickly piñata. I picked one up, and the label read lithium. My mother looked defeated. I said, "Don't worry, mommy, we're all just bags of chemicals in the

> end."

A passage from Courteney Cox's journal, found by Jennifer Aniston on the set of Friends, 1997

Lithium. I was just thinking of lithium. Of pills. Psychiatric medication.

Confront this synchronicity head on. Do not let it fester inside of you.

One more, I thought. Just one more, and I'll put the journal down after that. Maybe make a call to my old psychiatrist if it gets too bad. Get back on the pills if it gets out of hand. Yes, the pills. There are always the pills. Lithium, risperidone, clonazepam, and four others I can't remember. I continued reading.

> Dustin described my shoulder blade as *bletcherous*, or disgustingly designed. He could be mean in the morning, as he said this during what he called my *pandiculation*, or my act of stretching and yawning after waking up. He liked watching me get dressed in the morning, as he called himself a *tibialoconcupiscent*, or one who likes to watch women put on stockings. His love for esoteric words made him a *logolept*. He became a logolept right before the filming of Rain Man, where his deep method acting convinced him that he had a form of Savant Syndrome, like the autistic character Raymond he was playing. The original script had Raymond have an immense vocabulary. The last minute change to the script made him have an unusual

> talent for numbers and calculations instead. This script change was Dustin's greatest *hamartia.*

Lisa Hoffman speaking of her husband, Dustin Hoffman, to her psychologist, 1999

The towering image of the mildly autistic Fucko sprang back into my mind. And my psychiatrist? Dr. Hoffman of course. I couldn't help myself from turning the page.

> Paul's excitement that autumn morning was incredible. "Look at that young boy over there. He is a whirling dervish! He is performing dhikr, worshipping Allah. To think we have a member of the Mevlevi Order right here in Milford. Soon he will whirl into an ecstatic trance, his white skirt representing ego's shroud. Round and round he goes! He will remove his black cloak and be spiritually born into the truth. He is like a black and white blur, his spins so elegant." I interrupted, "Paul, that isn't a boy. That's two dalmatians humping. How much have you had to drink this morning?" Paul, taking a beat, replied, "Clearly not enough, for I also see two other young boys dancing the Tibetan Yak Dance."

Al Franken recounting a conversation with Paul Giamatti, 2014

It was funny, but I wasn't laughing. I turned to the television. A rerun of Cheers was playing. No Paul Giamatti. No Al Franken. No whirling dervishes, no Tibetan Yak Dances, and definitely no dalmatians humping. The young girl was looking at me again. I wiped the sweat from my brow and smirked a cancer smirk.

* * *

Relief. The relief I felt, I can't even describe. Twenty minutes. Naomi had only been in to see Dr. Reece for twenty minutes, and it almost all fell apart. I thought about the institution. About Sydney, Latonya, and William. *William*. When I first got there, after they removed my shoelaces, a young man with Down syndrome who I would later know as William jumped on me. He had a pair of scissors in his hand. I deftly pushed him off of me and ran up to the nearest tech and screamed, "There's some retarded guy trying to kill me!" The tech, a woman wearing cat eye glasses like a librarian scowled at me like, well, like a librarian.

"We don't use that word around here."

"But..."

I looked down at my laceless shoes and felt like a horrible person. Later on, during the mutiny, William would become my closest confidant. My top lieutenant.

I needed a smoke. I put on my coat and went downstairs to the busy sidewalk. I tripped into a man wearing a Connecticut Sun baseball cap and sunglasses. The glasses fell off, and I grabbed him to keep us both upright. Kneeling on the ground, I looked up at the man to make sure he was OK.

Fucking Paul Giamatti.

* * *

I went back upstairs to find Naomi finished with her appointment early, sitting where I had been sitting. *Strung Out on Plenitudes* was propped up on the seat beside her. I quickly went over and grabbed it without her seeing. I slipped it into the back of my jeans and rustled my coat to cover it.

"How'd it go?" I asked.

"It was fine. The leukemia is still leukemia. Hey, you ever noticed that Dr. Reece is the *spitting image* of Margaret Thatcher?"

3

Bazooka

Before I continue, and this might seem a bit odd, but I must impart to you that *Strung Out on Plenitudes* was not the first errant publication that I had ever come across. When I was eighteen, I found an unpublished draft copy of a poetry chapbook titled *Uzis and Lean and all of the Wars in Between* underneath my seat on the Greyhound bus I was taking from Fort Lauderdale to New York City. The foreword described it as a collection of love poems that were violent in nature. I committed every line of every poem to memory on that long bus ride so I could pick up pretty women at dive bars when I reached the city. I still remember them to this day. I ran into Fairuza Balk at one hole in the wall joint. The name escapes me. The first poem I recited to her went like this:

Your candy bead necklace
Got violently jacked
And snapped
With tiny munition sounds
As the beads hit the ground —

Syncopated clicks
Like Glocks
Being cocked
By the rest of the gang
Who stood by and watched
As you drew your bazooka
And obliterated the world
You, the most powerful girl

4

Extra Soy Sauce, Home Alone, Pat Morita

I didn't pick up the journal for a good three weeks. Naomi's hair was starting to thin from her second round of chemo. She needed me, so I took a few weeks off of work. I hid the journal in plain sight on our book shelf in between Murakami's *Norwegian Wood* and Pynchon's *The Crying of Lot 49*. Naomi wasn't a fan of either, so my secret yellow journal was safe there. I couldn't stop thinking about it. I was addicted, like a junkie. A junkie who was *Strung out on Plenitudes*. Ha.

Surprisingly, Naomi was always hungry. She would vomit most meals up, of course, but her appetite never waned.

"Where are we going tonight, my love?" I asked. "Mexico? China? Thailand? How about Ethiopia?"

"Tonight we are in Shanghai, sitting on a park bench in Lujiazui watching the Huangpu River flow by. I want moo goo gai pan."

"Extra soy sauce?" I asked

"No. Dr. Reece said too much salt can cause edema. My kidney numbers aren't looking so hot from the chemo. Want me to call the order in ahead?" she asked.

I eyed the bookshelf like I was in a western.

"No that's okay. I'll order there and have a beer while I'm waiting. Maybe catch up on some reading."

* * *

Grand Chinese Restaurant wasn't too far away, so I walked. My left hand was cold, pressing against the pulped cover of the journal. I traced my index finger in a back and forth motion over the uneven surface like a surfer bobbing on little waves while waiting for the big one to come. I was *excited.* Was that a sign of mania, I thought? My three weeks of abstinence from the journal made the anxiety over a possible breakdown go away. Far away. I picked up my pace into a light jog.

I ordered Naomi's moo goo gai pan and General Tso's tofu for me. I was a vegetarian for over three decades at this point, mind you. I still craved seafood but didn't miss meat or poultry. A waiter walked by with two plates of Kung Pao shrimp. I had never had it, as I became a vegetarian at a young age before I could try everything the ocean had to offer. It smelled great. I sat down at the bar.

I sipped on a Tsingtao, one of my favorite beers next to Kirin Ichiban. But that was a Japanese beer. We didn't have Japanese very often. The sushi was too tempting for me.

The restaurant was warm, so I took my sweater off. I was ready. I had my beer. I was cooling off. There was a good fifteen minutes I'd say until the food was ready. I opened the journal.

> Reading the fortune from the cookie, I uttered, "You learn from your mistakes, and you will learn a lot today." After we had sex, the delivery man tossed the condom and pulled up his pants. He said, "That'll be $12.95." I didn't know if I was paying for the moo goo gai pan or the sex. I gave him a twenty and told him to keep the change just in case it was both. The sex was worth about $3.00, and I left a $4.05 tip as he forgot the extra soy sauce. I usually tip more. I opened the second fortune cookie and read, "There is a prospect of a harrowing time ahead for you." I then realized that I opened the fortune cookies in the wrong order. Seeing my fatal flaw, I dared not use the chopsticks.

Halle Berry speaking to Eartha Kitt on the set of Boomerang, as overheard by Eddie Murphy, 1991

It was good. Not Margaret Thatcher good. But good nonetheless. Naturally, I asked the tiny woman tending the bar for a fortune cookie. This was fun, I thought. I was feeling calm. No harm, no foul. I moved onto the next.

> There was nothing else to be done. I took horny goat weed picked from the garden and steeped it in Koshary tea. I took a sip and accidentally spilled it all over my my bare lap. There, in the tea leaves on the floor, it read:
>
> 'Nothing is as good or bad as it appears. It is better to

> be alone sometimes.'
>
> I took off the condom, sent her home, and ordered Chinese food just to read the fortune cookies. I realized that everything, both good and bad, comes gift-wrapped in goddamn mysticism. It was not the Christmas I was hoping for.

Macaulay Culkin to Mel Gibson, 2009

Moo goo gai pan. Fortune cookies. Extra soy sauce. I bet there was a condom vending machine in the bathroom. On a whim, I decided to check. I downed the little bit of beer that was left in the bottle.

Indeed there was! It was old and rusty, like an unrestored 1950s gas station pump. There was a man using one of the filthy urinals, his left hand holding his penis and his right swatting at flies. He was skinny and short, but he held his penis as if it were a barbell. Like he needed both hands, but the flies were just too much. There were so many flies, you'd think you were in some kind of Alfred Hitchcock movie.

I went to the sink and splashed some water on my face. I looked at the dirty mirror. Yup, it was me alright. This was really happening. I smiled. I was giddy, even.

I went back to the bar and ordered another Tsingtao. I could feel imaginary flies behind my ears and in my nostrils. I swatted out of habit, but there were no flies at the bar. I opened the journal back up.

> Most people don't know this about The Karate Kid, but the scene where Pat Morita and I were trying to catch flies with chopsticks was written into the script at the last minute. The scene was inspired by Pat's actual hobby of catching flies with chopsticks. You should have seen him by the craft service table, giddy as a school boy, yelling "Come here you little motherfuckers!" He was such a great man. He held me as I cried over not getting the role of Holden Caulfield in an off-Broadway production of *The Catcher in the Rye.* Pat was a lot of things, but a goddamn phony he was not.

Ralph Macchio's forward to his unpublished biography of Pat Morita, tentatively titled "The Fly Catcher in the Rye"

The food was ready. My beer bottles were empty. The fun was over. The tiny woman tending the bar never brought me a fortune cookie. It was time to go home.

5

Beretta

When we got to Fairuza's place, she wanted to hear more of the poetry I had found on the bus. I pretended I had written the first poem, so I had to continue the ruse. I could see where this was going, so I recited a less innocent, more sensual, and highly weaponized piece as she mixed the drinks with a cherry red lipstick-stained straw:

We lie on a heart-shaped bed
That is covered in
One thousand 9mm shells
While a mirrored ceiling
Hangs shattered
As we are aimless, your
Ruger and
My Beretta
Sensually magazined
Like the catastrophe
Of our bodies
As lovers

Holstered deep into the night

6

Asana Tea Party, Textual Asemia, Sisyphus Kink

We were in the city for Naomi to do her cancer yoga. There was a place called Oncology Yoga not too far from the Museum of Modern Art, and we were going to make a day out of it. We were sitting in the lobby, watching sick women do yoga and waiting for Naomi's class to begin. I was high on some of Naomi's Oxycodone for her gallbladder. The gallbladder needed to be removed, but due to the complications from her chemo, she couldn't have the surgery just yet. We'd see what her hemoglobin levels looked like at her next appointment with Dr. Reece.

Now look. I'm not a drug addict. I just like getting high every now and then. I've never been addicted to anything other than cigarettes and black coffee. And I've done every drug I could get my hands on. I've tried it all. PCP, heroin, and so on. I never tried crack, but that was a gentrification thing and just a matter of not having access to it. I think every white person is at least a little bit racist, and I'd estimate I was about 5% racist. Not too bad.

Naomi and I would drop acid every three months or so and go to Times Square to gaze at the tourists. We were about four months overdue because of the leukemia. What a shame, I thought.

We had heard about Oncology Yoga from Dr. Reece, and Naomi reluctantly agreed to try it. She found it all to be a bit 'woo woo'—alternative therapies and the such. This wasn't alternative therapy, Dr. Reece insisted. It was *complimentary* therapy.

So I sat there, on drugs and thinking about drugs, waiting for Naomi to start her class so I could continue reading the yellow journal. It was in my messenger bag, still a secret to Naomi.

"OK, my class is starting. Thanks for coming with me today," she said.

"Of course, my love." I patted her tush as she stood up and gave her a wink.

* * *

It had been three days since I visited Grand Chinese Restaurant. Three days since I opened the journal.

I opened it gently, with a smirk. I shared smirks with *Strung Out on Plenitudes* now. I'm sure it would smirk back at me if it had a mouth.

> You practice your yoga vinyasas to better transition between your asana sitting meditation poses. This is much to my delight, as I find meditation very erotic

> when performed in the padmasana or sitting lotus position. Legs crossed and palms up, I imagine seven more of you here for perhaps an orgy. Or to have a tea party. Or even to sit in a circle to play duck duck goose. Speaking of ducks, you can now transition to the karandavasana, better known as the Himalayan duck pose. With your face down and ass up, that's the way we like to fuck. Fuck fuck goose! God, I love PCP.

Kelsey Grammer to his wife Kayte Walsh, 2019

I laughed a few decibels too loud, and the girl at the front desk looked up from her phone and hushed me with her eyes. She was pretty, with a long thin face and small ears revealed by a turquoise headband. I wondered if she had cancer too. I continued my reading.

> Is this supposed to be asemic writing in your handsome Moleskin notebook? You know, where the script looks like handwriting but in fact has no meaning or infinite meaning depending on the observer? Or is it just chicken scratch? Asemic writing can perhaps get you a show here at the MoMA. But if this is indeed chicken scratch, dear girl, then how can you expect Eazy-E to look down from heaven and read your dope rhymes? Oh, and did that blotter paper taste weird to you?

Jeff Goldblum to Fairuza Balk at the Museum of Modern Art, NYC, 2010

Ah, Fairuza. I thought about that night again. About my other secret book, *Uzis and Lean and all of the Wars in Between.* I wonder what ever happened to it? Maybe I would find it again one day, under the seat on another bus. Or perhaps an airplane. I recited one of its poems in my head, silently moving my lips.

She sleeps
With a stuffed axolotl
And an an Avtomat Kalashnikova
Because he is at the public house
And dreams are censure
And violence

It was weird, a stuffed axolotl. Nobody really knew about axolotls back then a little over three decades ago. They weren't in the zeitgeist. And stuffed axolotl plushies, well, they definitely weren't a thing like they are now. Oh well. I reached into Naomi's purse and took another Oxycodone. I turned the page.

> Everyone loves the story of Sisyphus pushing the boulder uphill as a metaphor for the human condition. But what if he just liked pushing things? Or maybe he had a boulder kink. I like doing heroin. It doesn't have to speak to the depth of pain and self-medicating nature of whatever-the-fuck. I just like getting high, man. Now leave me alone. I've got a boulder to push and a pusher to meet.

Philip Seymour Hoffman speaking at his intervention, 2013

I looked up to the sound of someone vomiting. It was Naomi. Her yoga mat was ruined. How embarrassed she must feel, I thought. The MoMA would be there tomorrow, I told her. She was crying when we got back on the PATH train to Hoboken.

7

Grasping at my Penis, Starboard, Deeper than the Asthenosphere, Paint it Black

About five minutes into the train ride back to Hoboken, Naomi was sound asleep. I wondered if cancer made you dream differently. I made a mental note to ask her that later when she was feeling better. Careful not to disturb her, I rustled around in my messenger bag for the journal. I had a little time to kill before our stop.

> For ten minutes on the PATH train, I was a synesthete. My signals got crossed from either leaving Hoboken for the last time or entering New York City for the first time. I noticed that the train smelled like cyan and sounded like 137. A Mexican woman was breastfeeding, and her blouse slipped, showing me her full bosom. I tried not to stare, but it was so delicious, her right breast tasting like peaches and her left tasting like cream. I thought I was caught in a dream, and I reached down my pants, grasping at my penis. I was always

> losing my penis in dreams. I knew I was awake when I felt my penis, and it felt like the song *Chain of Fools* by Aretha Franklin.

Nathan Lane speaking to his neurologist, 1973

For a brief moment a twinge of sadness enveloped me. What was I going to do when I was finished with *Strung Out on Plenitudes*? I so looked forward to stealing these brief little moments away from Naomi. Away from the cancer.

The walk to the train was cold, and my lips were chapped. I grabbed some lip balm out of Naomi's purse. It tasted like peaches and cream. We were almost at our stop. I had time for one more.

> The caverns in your chapped lips are as deep as the Kuril-Kamchatka Trench in the Pacific. The Kraken could emerge at anytime. Submersibles dare not to enter. Oh, the great sea battles that must have been fought on your lips! Odysseus and his Homeric galleys would stand no chance. And, indeed, I do not envy the voyage your herpes must undertake during a breakout. Avast!

Former President Bill Clinton to an anonymous woman, 2002

Great. Now I had to worry about having herpes. This day couldn't get much worse. The train stopped, and I shook Naomi awake. When I stepped out to the aisle, I accidentally kicked something from under the seat. It was a journal. A black one. I picked it up. It was titled *My Time at the Institution: An Autobiography.* I slid it into my bag, because that's what you do when you find your autobiography that you never wrote.

This day had gotten much worse.

* * *

On the walk home my head hurt. Everything was fuzzy. I couldn't complain because, well, because my girlfriend had leukemia. I wondered if they had support groups for people with girlfriends that have leukemia. I know they had them for cancer, but that was too general. I like organizations that are very specific. I needed one specifically for people with *girlfriends that have leukemia.* I mean, Narcotics Anonymous? Which narcotics? Anonymous who? They needed to be pinpointed like a laser. Like, they needed to have one for aunts who smoke sherms. Aunts who smoke sherms have different needs than ballet dancers who snort crystal meth. Wasn't that obvious to anyone? God my head hurt.

Did I just really find an autobiographical account of my time at the institution that I didn't write?

"You OK, hon?" Naomi asked.

I lit a cigarette. "I'm fine."

"You sure don't look fine. Want another Oxy? Sorry about ruining our day."

"No, it's fine." I said as we passed by a mini-mart. "Hey, do we have anything in the house for dinner? I don't feel like getting take out."

"I don't think so. I'll run in real quick and get something.

Maybe some soup for my stomach," she replied.

She was almost inside when I called out, "Can you get me something sweet? Like some Tootsie Pops?"

"Sure!"

I leaned against the wall of the mini-mart and opened my messenger bag to grab the journal. Not my brand new autobiography. The yellow journal.

> So I was returning to LA from Miami, and I just so happened to be seated next to George Foreman. As you know, I am a nervous flyer, and I was going through Tootsie Pops like I was chain smoking. George was cool as a cucumber during the turbulence, and it comforted me. To break the ice, I said "Hey George, do you know how many licks it takes to get to the center of a Tootsie Pop?" He replied, "Well, young man, it depends on where you think the center begins. Let's say we are talking about the Earth. Are you talking about the the mantle, the outer core, or the inner core?" I let out a nervous giggle and answered, "Um... the chocolate part?" He looked at me both shocked and dead serious. "The inner core? You son of a bitch, don't you know we'll be burned alive?" Panicked, he got up and whispered something to the flight attendant. I was quickly restrained, and when we landed I was dragged off the plane by the police. That's how I got put on the no-fly list.

Jared Leto to his publicist, 2022

She'll be out soon, I thought. But surely I had enough time for one more?

> So you say that the mystery flavor of Dum Dum lollipops is your favorite, huh? Oh boy do I have news for you. The flavor is different every time. It's a result of the end of one batch of a normal flavor mixing with the beginning of a new batch of a normal flavor. It can't be your favorite. It's just a random mishmash from an uncleaned machine during the manufacturing process. Son, you are such a *sucker*. And don't call that a dad joke. I'm not your real father.

Mick Jagger to Deveraux Jagger, 2023

Naomi came out just as I was putting the journal back into my bag.

"They didn't have any Tootsie Pops so I got you a bag of Dum Dums. Is that OK?" she asked.

"That's fine." I lit another cigarette. "Honey, does cancer make you dream differently?"

"Hmm. I don't think so. I don't really remember my dreams these days," she said.

"Oh," I replied.

The sun was setting a nice shade of purple with pink highlights. We didn't talk the rest of the walk home.

8

Mortar Shell

I sensed Fairuza was getting bored of me over amaretto sours. Her eyes only lit up when I was reciting these damn poems. I decided to bring out something a bit more gory. She seemed like the type of girl who liked gore, or at least she was typecast as one:

A dapper sailor boy
In his sailor suit
Carried a mortar shell
To the Sadie Hawkins dance
Cause he didn't stand a chance,
But Grace's wandering eyes
Maimed all the other guys
So she brought him a soda pop
And they danced
Over the scattered bodies
Of the other sailor boys
In June of '44
A blood-soaked dance floor

9

Quantity Obsessions, Tozan and Forest, Consolation Prize, Hopi Prophecies

Something about *Strung Out on Plenitudes* was making me a little cocksure. I found a book roughly the same dimensions as the yellow journal, Julio Cortázar's *Hopscotch* to be exact, expertly cut the cover off of it, and affixed it to the yellow journal. Now, I could read it anywhere, as long as eyes weren't too prying. I did this when Naomi was sleeping the night before, glue stick and all. Now, I was on the couch in the living room, and I cracked it open. At that very second Naomi came out of the bedroom, and I instinctively slid it under a pillow, completely disregarding my expert camouflage. This would take some getting used to, I thought — my newfound freedom.

"What time are we leaving?" I asked.

"We have to be there by seven." she said. "I haven't even figured out what I'm going to wear, and my dad is going to be so pissed if we're late."

We had tickets to see Penn and Teller.

"You look good," she said.

"Don't I know it," I said smiling, adjusting my tie. "How are you feeling?"

As the words were coming out of my mouth I realized something terrible. I didn't really care how she was feeling. One minute she was feeling good, the next bad. Happy then nauseous. Hungry then faint. It was all a big blur, so what did it matter how she felt? She would just change her damn mind in twenty minutes.

"A little nauseous," she said.

"Want me to run downstairs and pick up some ginger ale?" What was I doing? I didn't need excuses anymore to read my journal. I really hoped that she would say no.

"No, that's OK. I'll be fine."

Exactly, I thought. Give it twenty minutes and she'll be fine. I looked at my watch as if to time it.

"OK, I'm going to go find something to wear," she said. I smiled at her as she went back into the bedroom. I opened the journal.

> I know you think I am obsessed with quantities, but there are about 160,000 species of moths in the world compared to about 17,500 species of butterflies. Flamboyance is rarer than things that are unostentatious. I'm not trying to upset you darling, but you simply cannot pull off that dress. You can primp and preen all you want, but the sequins are pinching little parts of your breasts, and I can see these little mountains of flesh extruding from the spaces in between. I approximate there are about 600 itsy bitsy little bitty titty flesh mountains on your chest.

George Clooney to Amal Clooney, 2024

She came out of the bedroom quickly. Too quickly. She was in tears. She had on my favorite dress, and it looked ridiculous on her. She had lost so much weight. It's like we both forgot that she was throwing up every damn five minutes. Her breasts though, they still looked as fantastic as ever, peeking out of the sides of the ill-fitting dress. I guess that was a consolation prize, I thought.

"It's your favorite dress," she sobbed.

Trying to lighten the mood, I said, "Well, you certainly don't have your mother's figure."

She sniffed in some snot and giggled. Her mother was morbidly obese. She went back into the room. I picked the journal back up.

> There is a Buddhist koan that you should know if you're going to continue to ask me these silly questions. It goes something like this:
>
> A monk asked Tozan when he was weighing some flax, "What is Buddha?" Tozan said, "This flax weighs three pounds."
>
> So when you come to me asking epistemological nonsense like, "What is love?" the only answer I can give you is, "Your mom weighs 325 pounds."

Forest Whitaker to Jaye Davidson during a press junket for The Crying Game, 1992

She came back out of the bedroom with another silly-looking dress on.

"Do you have anything that will fit? Maybe we can stop by Elisa's house on the way and you can borrow something?" I asked. Her friend, Elisa, was bulimic. God, I'd hate to see those two at a buffet, gorging and purging in unison, I thought.

She wiped more snot from her nose and said, "I'll call her to see if she's home. She went back into the bedroom. I continued reading.

> "I just love unicorns. Why are they called that?" Anna Nicole asked. "Well, the meaning of words can be found in what's called etymology. The first part of the word, *uni*, means one. Unicorns have one horn," I replied. "Oh," she said with confidence. "Are there more parts of words like *uni* that mean one?" I smiled at her comprehension. I was proud even. "Sure, take *mono* for example. That means one as well. And then you have parts of words, like *bi*, that mean two." She jumped up as if a literal lightbulb went off in a void. She said, "So *pen* means one and *testic* means two. I get it!" I looked at her breasts as a consolation prize and said, "Sure darling. Sure."

J. Howard Marshall II writing of his marriage to Anna Nicole Smith, 1994

Now she was throwing up in the bathroom. I looked at my watch and thought, she'll be fine in twenty minutes. I glanced back down at the journal.

> We were halfway through Koyaanisqatsi on VHS when Teller vomited. The smell of his vomit made me purge as well. I don't understand why people participate in ayahuasca ceremonies these days when the Qatsi Trilogy is now available on Blu-ray. The film itself is a trip, and communal vomiting doesn't have to be a sacred ritual. I find communal vomiting purists to be pretentious and rather obtuse.

Penn Jillette discussing film theory with Oprah Winfrey, 2017

We weren't late to the show. God those guys got old, I thought.

10

Semtex

Fairuza sat next to me on the couch, her eyes wanting more from me. Maybe these poems were written just for her? I sent out a volley:

You wouldn't do that to me
Even in a movie
Or a song
But maybe in a book
That the fascists would burn
As their tender hearts would break
From the title alone
The prelude all Semtex
The epilogue an atomic bomb

11

Dunce Cap, Carcosa, Female Water Hare

Confident? Independent? I'm not sure. Every time I had a chance to read *Strung Out on Plenitudes* I felt more like I did when I was younger. Like when I picked up Fairuza Balk at some hole in the wall joint I can't remember the name of in the city. Bold, maybe. Yes, bold. I didn't dare open the black journal, *My Time at the Institution: An Autobiogaphy,* though. I might have been feeling like I was young again, but my constitution still wouldn't allow it. A week prior, I had hidden it on the bookshelf it in between Calvino's *Cosmicomics* and Self's *My Idea of Fun.* Naomi didn't like those books, so she would never go near them. As a matter of fact, I couldn't remember the last book Naomi liked. She was sitting on the couch watching The Real Housewives of Salt Lake City. When did she start watching this nonsense? I was on the toilet with my journal.

> I tried to study Speculative Realism, specifically Object-Oriented Ontology, but then I met you. To think your lips existed without me kissing them was too much to

> bear. Now I am addicted to The Real Housewives of Salt Lake City. I thought it was a scripted show rooted in magical realism. Sometimes I am a real idiot, and my head is too big for the dunce cap.

David Letterman to his wife Regina Lasko on their anniversary, 2021

I heard vomiting coming from the living room. Goddamn it, I thought. I wasn't going to do it this time. I was not going to jump off the toilet and go tend to her. She should be used to vomiting by now, right? She should have the whole ordeal under control after so much practice. She could enter the Vomiting Olympics and at least take home a bronze.

> "It was crazy, man. It was about a month ago. One minute I'm rehearsing my lines for the Yellow King scene, and the next minute I'm on the floor having a full blown seizure, abnormal neuronal firing and all. I was shaking uncontrollably, man. It was a trip," Matthew said. Woody replied, "Yeah in '07 I had a seizu-" Matthew cut him off abruptly with, "Woo-hoo, look at me. I'm Woody Harrelson, and I had a seizure five years before Matthew McConaughey! I'm a seizure hipster! Everyone look, I had a seizure way before Matthew McConaughey did, before it was cool to have seizures. I bet you smoke your weed at 4:19 too, just to beat everyone to the punch, huh? Woo-hoo! Look everyone, I'm Woody Harrelson, and I lit my joint before you did. Woo-hoo!"

A conversation between Matthew McConaughey and Woody Harrelson as overheard by Michelle Monaghan on the set of True Detective, 2013

I propped myself up on our bed and pretended I couldn't hear her from the bedroom. I turned the television on, and True Detective was playing, of course. Over a decade later, and it still held up as one of the greatest detective shows of all time. I finished the episode and went into the living room to check on Naomi.

"I thought you'd never get out of the bathroom," she said, carrying her vomit bowl to the kitchen.

"I told you to stop at one burger," I said. Her eating had gotten absolutely out of control. And it all went to waste, coming out the wrong end. Don't you know there are starving children in Africa, I wanted to ask her. What a stupid saying. There were starving children all over the world. It wasn't all just Black babies with bloated stomachs. That was reductionist. See? Only 5% racist.

I sat down on the couch to read.

> It's the Tibetan New Year! Let's dance the Tibetan Yak Dance like the Mahayana sect of Buddhist Tribes of Arunachal Pradesh do. You can be the yak, and I'll mount you. It's the year of the Male Wood Dragon, so let's rejoice! Last year's celebration was a bad time, as I was in the processes of self-negation and sick on too many yak burgers. Actually, maybe I should be the yak, and you can mount me this year, for I have already had five yak burgers and can feel my tummy rumbling. We don't want a repeat of the year of the Female Water Hare, when I pooped my pants all over Tobey Maguire.

Andrew Garfield to Tom Holland, 2024

The coincidences didn't faze me at all anymore. It had become commonplace. I wouldn't have even mentioned them at a dinner party. I had total control. I was strong. I had once even picked up *Fairuza Balk* at some hole in the wall joint I can't remember the name of in the city. Even if we didn't sleep together, that was still an accomplishment. But what if we had? What if I had picked a different poem before she asked me to leave? And she got pregnant? I would have a child with Fairuza Balk, now, already out of college with a thriving career in Hollywood. Fairuza's connections and all. And nobody would be vomiting. I had a strict rule about no vomiting in our mansion in the Hollywood Hills.

12

Brass Knuckles

Fairuza smiled and asked for more, inching closer to me and removing the pillow that separated us. I felt vulnerable, so I recited vulnerability:

Hopscotch and
Hand grenades,
Holding my hand
With brass knuckles,
To be twelve again
And riding a roller coaster
Off the coast of Normandy,
Bastogne in the winter
When we dug trenches
To play hopscotch

13

Sid and Nancy - Part 1

I was at the drugstore picking up some snacks for Naomi. The drugstore was closer than the supermarket, and all she wanted was junk food anyway. I was checking out, and the line was almost out the door. The young man at the register was a snail. He even wore his hair like a snail, a beanie draped over his mullet. The older lady in front of me smelled like patchouli. The man behind me was a bulldog, short and thick with no neck to speak of. It was quite a scene. I slipped my journal out of my messenger bag.

> Look, this one is different this time. Half green and half orange. Isn't it pretty? And it's a capsule now, not a tablet. The green and orange will melt away in my stomach and release chemical power. Is it true what you said? That we're all just bags of chemicals? I take so many types these days, fistfuls even. The blue ovals and pink circles are my favorite. They remind me of pregnancy. Do you think they will let me take my

> pharmaceutical fistfuls when I'm pregnant? Do you think they will ever let me get pregnant? Momma? Are you still listening? Momma, please.

Nancy Spungen to her mother, six years before meeting Sid Vicious.

Damn, I thought. Naomi must have had a prescription waiting that I forgot about. I stepped out of the line and went over to the pharmacy counter.

"Hey there," I said to Cindy. I was on a first name basis with the pharmacist at this point. Cindy even baked cookies for Naomi one time. She had a kind smile like a foreign grandmother you would see in a National Geographic magazine.

"Here for Naomi, hon?"

"You know it."

"Ok, let me check the computer," she said as she put on the reading glasses she had hanging around her neck.

"I don't have anything here for her. Which medication are you looking for?"

I didn't answer. I was in shock. That is until I saw the pregnancy tests on the shelf to my right.

* * *

I bought a pregnancy test and left the drugstore, forgetting Naomi's snacks. Not that it was necessary. She was pregnant. *Strung Out on Plenitudes* had told me so. It was particularly cold out, and I was chain smoking on the walk home. The sides of my vision were blurry.

What do they do when pregnant women have leukemia, I thought. They must have science for that. They have science for everything these days. Science that nobody knows about except for the scientists. Science you only learn about when you need to learn about it. Like when your girlfriend has leukemia and is pregnant. I bet they have support groups for it even. It must be common enough for science to have figured the whole situation out by now. Common enough for it to have support groups.

* * *

I got home, and Naomi wasn't there. I had forgotten it was her Oncology Yoga day. She was in the city. I sat down on the couch to read, but I couldn't concentrate. All I could think about was scientists and test tubes. A room with chairs arranged in a circle, coffee and stale donuts on the table. A baby with no Hollywood connections like Fairuza had.

14

Ilavaluthi

I could tell that the last one didn't fit the mood. Fairuza wanted undisturbed violence. She wanted explosions:

Your undetonated Ilavaluthi
On which I play jacks
Will leave me
Unpelvised
Despined
My mine detector Mark I
As useless
As my legless
Heart

15

Minkowski Space

So Naomi died. Not of the cancer, but by a hit and run when she was crossing the street to go to Oncology Yoga. They didn't tell me if she was pregnant or not. I'm not sure what the protocol is for that sort of thing. Reading my journal on the train ride home from Mount Sinai Hospital, I thought of Fairuza and all of those poems.

> My heart doesn't beat; it throbs. I think that is how the poem started. It was rubbish meant for those who'd rather be clever than be loved. A true heart doesn't beat or throb. It tap dances through the three dimensions of space and the one dimension of time into a single four-dimensional continuum. That continuum is what we call spacetime, or Minkowski space, darling. A true heart shuffles, flaps, stamps, and heel drops through Minkowski space. I know I was rough on that rubbish poem, but I'd rather be harsh than gentle. Speaking of which, I don't remember our safe word, and I can't

> hear anything you are saying through that ball gag. Enough about poems, hearts, and spacetime. It's time for me to whip that ass.

Rita Wilson to Tom Hanks, 2016

16

Morning Star

Fairuza blushed and kissed me on the forehead. She then, inexplicably, and I mean with no warning, slapped me in the face and asked me to leave. Oh her duality! Thirty minutes later I was on the L train to Brooklyn to visit a friend, and I recited one last poem from the chapbook to myself:

You brought a morning star
To a Friday night fistfight
And LARPed medieval
To my heart-like palpitations
Of punches
So sincere —
Your soda can tab chainmail
Protecting
Your innocence
As I dreamed
Of a chivalrous fuck

II

Part Two

My Time at the Institution: An Autobiography

17

The Oligarch of Cincinnati, Sinistrophobia, Radio Raheem

Still on the train ride home from Mount Sinai Hospital, I glanced over to a crippled Black man with a very stylish fade siting across from to me. Even on this train ride home, I couldn't escape sickness. Naomi was dead, and now I had to deal with deformity. I opened the journal.

> Before I got into acting, I took almost any job I could find. One year, I got a gig answering telephones at the The Jerry Lewis MDA (Muscular Dystrophy Association) Labor Day Telethon. About five minutes into the marathon, I picked up a call, and an old raspy voice asked, "How much do I have to pledge to get these wretched deformed things off of my television set? I can't find my remote control to change the channel." At first I thought it was a prank, but the caller was insistent on speaking to my superior. I handed the phone to my manager, and in 30 seconds

> her face turned white. I asked who it was on the phone. She said I wouldn't believe her if she told me. There was a big commotion backstage. I overheard all of the bigwigs crunching numbers and doing a cost-benefit analysis. Let's just say that WKRC-TV in Cincinnati had technical difficulties broadcasting the marathon that year, and it was replaced by M*A*S*H reruns. I eventually did find out who the man on the phone was, but you wouldn't believe me if I told you.

Angela Bassett to Samuel L. Jackson on the set of Chi-Raq, 2014

The man's right hand clearly didn't work, so he was sketching something in his notebook with his left. I kept on reading.

> My mother has sinistrophobia. Her deep-seated fear of anything involving the left-hand side includes left-handed people, like me, her son. I didn't know this until I found a haiku she wrote when she was drunk one Sunday afternoon:
>
> *When I see lefties*
> *Writing, I get grossed out at*
> *Their palsied motions*
>
> And yet she loves me so dearly. I love my mother as much as she hates smudged ink on paper.

Keanu Reeves speaking to Al Pacino on the set of The Devil's Advocate, 1996

Why was I so nonplussed about Naomi's death? About our little cancer baby? Was it *Strung Out on Plenitudes*? Is that why I had found the journal in the first place? To prepare me for my girlfriend dying? To detach myself from the mundane everyday reality of being someone with a girlfriend with leukemia?

In the short time I had been reading the journal, my mood had changed. I was more like my younger self. Confident. Less emotional. Nonchalant. Without attachments. Certainly less attached to Naomi and her cancer. I had nothing to mourn when I was eighteen on the bus ride up to the city as my younger self. Maybe mourning was now something I wouldn't feel anymore. I would have to playact to her friends and family.

"Hey, what are you drawing?" I asked the deformed man.

"You," he said.

"Oh wow, that's pretty awesome," I said, switching seats to sit next to him. He was very talented.

"I like to draw sad things."

"I'm sad? Why do you think that?"

"You might not know it, but you are a very sad man," he added. "It's not like I see it in your eyes. You have very vacant eyes. It's more in your posture. The way you sit reading your journal. You have a profound sadness in you."

"Well, my girlfriend did just die," I said.

"When?"

"Just now. A few hours ago."

"No, that's not it. This sadness is older. About eight years older, I'd say."

Eight years? Why was he so specific? Eight years ago would make it 2017. When I was institutionalized. Had I found an oracle on the PATH train to Hoboken? I had read that some cultures viewed physical deformities as a sign of spiritual calling.

* * *

"This is my stop," I said. "This might seem weird, but do you want to grab a beer? My girlfriend did just die and all. I could use the company."

"I don't drink, but I'd very much like to finish this drawing of you," he replied.

We took a cab over to Naomi's and my favorite dive bar, Wilton House. We didn't speak in the cab. He was the very definition of a passenger, staring out of his window solemnly.

I ordered a Pabst Blue Ribbon, and he ordered an orange juice. We sat in silence for a while at the bar as he continued to sketch me. I didn't want to disturb him, so I opened my journal. *Fight the Power* by Public Enemy was playing in the background. I really loved that song. It made me nostalgic.

> When I was in high school, I once wrote a comparative essay between Jane Austin's *Persuasion* and Spike Lee's *Do the Right Thing*. My teacher did not like the section on Captain Frederick Wentworth and Radio Raheem where I wrote about love and hate and their affects on the libido. She marked the paper all in red, the same red hue as the lingerie she wore when she would make me recite Rainer Maria Rilke poems to her. We always made love while *Fight the Power* by Public Enemy played on the boombox in her bedroom. It was not as erotic as it sounds.

Jake Gyllenhaal to Heath Ledger on the set of Brokeback Mountain as overheard by Ang Lee, 2004

I finished my beer, and he finished his orange juice.

"I'm done with the drawing," he said, holding it up in front of me.

It definitely was me, and indeed, there was a profound sadness to it. It was haunting, like a Francis Bacon.

"What happened to you eight years ago?" he asked.

"You have some time?"

"Sure. I have nowhere to be," he said, closing his notebook. "Tonight is my drawing night. I wander around and draw sad things."

"Let's go back to my apartment. I have something to show you."

18

Pruinescence, Of Amphibians and Bad Habits, Blunted Instruments, Nocturnal Emissions

Back at my apartment, it felt like the lights were off even though they were on. *My* apartment, not *our* apartment. Naomi's ill-fitted dresses were draped over a kitchen table chair. Her basket of pill bottles sat next to the toaster oven on the messy kitchen counter. What was I going to do with all of these pill bottles? There must be a service that disposes of pill bottles belonging to the dead. They have services for everything these days. I even heard of a service where you could rent a friend for the day. *My friends*, I thought. *Naomi's friends. Our friends.* I had to call them. Tell them the big news.

I hadn't asked my palsied friend his name, but it felt like it was too late now. We had already shared a mysticism.

"Can I get you something to drink? I asked.

"Do you have any O.J.?"

"I sure do," I said, jovially. I was happy he was here. It felt like I was preparing ayahuasca for a ceremony that we were about to perform. I poured two glasses of orange juice and added a healthy amount of vodka to mine.

"Where is your bathroom?" he asked after he downed his glass of O.J. in one gulp. This guy really liked his O.J.

I showed him to the bathroom and opened my journal for a quickie.

> I had a dream that I was a powdered dancer. The damselfly I mean. Not an actual powdered dancer. If I was an actual powdered dancer, I wouldn't have been able to land on the tip of your nose, you silly girl. And what did you do in my dream? You sneezed. I mean what else is a silly girl to do in this type of situation? Squash me into your face? If you had, I would have said it was a nightmare, not a dream. Don't you listen to me anymore? Silly girl, why don't you listen to me anymore? Is it because I cross my heart and hope to die, stick a needle in my eye did not kill your mother?

O.J. Simpson speaking to his daughter, Sydney Brooke Simpson, 1995

My new friend came out of the bathroom, and I motioned him to the La-Z-Boy. He sat down and held the sketch book on his lap. I got up from the couch and retrieved *My Time at the Institution: An Autobiography* from the book shelf and handed it to him. I accidentally moved it towards his right hand, the one that clearly didn't work, and he awkwardly grabbed it with his left.

"You wanted to know what happened to me eight years ago."

"Yes, it was a very sad thing," he replied.

"Well, this is an autobiography that I didn't write that explains the whole thing," I said.

"An autobiography that you didn't write? I don't understand."

"Me neither," I said. "I want you to take it with you, and read it if you are so inclined."

"Have you read it?" he asked.

"No."

"Why not?"

"I already know what's in it. It *is* my autobiography after all."

* * *

My palsied friend had left. You'd think I'd be exhausted, but I wasn't. I felt free and *young*. In youth we are never exhausted, or so I remembered. I sifted through my vinyl collection for something to fit the mood. Neil Young? No, too folksy. Ah, this will do, I thought, as I pulled the Leonard Cohen record out from its sleeve. I put on *Sisters of Mercy*, sat down on the couch, and opened my journal.

> I was outside smoking when the Pacific giant salamander waddled up to me. It barked at me, as if chastising my habit. She was inside listening to Neil Young on the ancient record player, and no salamanders were there to tell her to stop. I don't know if she made it to *Harvest Moon* before she drank the Drano. I bet she did. Goddamn Neil Young. It should have been

> Leonard Cohen, but I shattered all of his records years before. During the first incident. The Pacific chorus frog incident.

Iggy Pop speaking of his time with an anonymous friend to Frank Black, as overheard by J Mascis, 1996

Salamanders. I thought of axolotls. Of William Shatner. Of the the young girl with cancer. I wondered if she had died yet. I switched records to Johnny Cash.

> The teleology of this saw is to cut wood. Not lignum vitae, the hardest of woods, but rather the balsa wood my father used to make model aircraft from. This saw is old and rusted with dampened teeth. The teleology of this saw is to cut soft woods. Here son, I give this saw to you. It will bring you much frustration and splinters. The teleology of this saw is to teach you about the pain of life, not the tree of life. Your mother will teach you about that in dreams, long after we both are dead. It shouldn't be long now.

Johnny Cash to his son John Carter Cash, 2003.

I had taken a couple of Naomi's Oxycodones. I guess they were my Oxycodones now. Between the pills and the vodka, I was finally starting to feel tired. I mean, I had gone through quite an ordeal, and I needed sleep.

> I've never told you this, but I'm obsessed with sleep disorders. Parasomnias. Hypnogely, somniloquy, somnambulism, all of them. Some would even call it a fetish. I have one you should know about. Stop with that look, it's not sexsomnia. I'm being serious. Sometimes when I'm falling asleep, I hear a sudden loud noise that makes me jump right out of bed. It's a horrible yet exciting auditory hallucination. My somnologist calls it exploding head syndrome. Stop smirking and get your mind out of the gutter. This is not what I had in mind for our wedding night, you hypnic jerk. Ba dum tss. Why aren't you laughing? Darling? Fine, I'm going to sleep.

Salma Hayek to her husband François-Henri Pinault, 2009

I went to the bedroom and lay down on the bed. This was the first time I would sleep alone in God knows how many years. I wished I had a profound thought about it, but I didn't. I just drifted to sleep.

19

William, at the Institution

When I first got committed, after they removed my shoelaces, a young man with Down syndrome who I would later know as William jumped on me. He had a pair of scissors in his hand. I deftly pushed him off of me and ran up to the nearest tech and screamed, "There's some retarded guy trying to kill me!" The tech, a woman wearing cat eye glasses like a librarian scowled at me like, well, like a librarian.

"We don't use that word around here."

"But..."

I looked down at my laceless shoes and felt like a horrible person. Later on, during the mutiny, William would become my closest confidant. My top lieutenant.

William had calmed down and approached me again.

"Do you want to see my poetry?" he asked.

"Sure," I said.

"I write poetry about Jesus"

"That's nice."

He guided me to a table that looked like it was made for

children and opened up a notebook. It was about a hundred pages of Jesus poetry written all in blue and green crayons. The poetry was all in blue except that every mention of Jesus was written in green. Why crayons, I wondered. As if reading my mind, William said, "They only let us have crayons here. For our safety. I'm William by the way."

"William, I have a question to ask you." I said. "If they are so concerned about our safety, how did you get your hands on the scissors?"

William looked to the right, then to the left. He whispered, "People underestimate me because I am special. I have my ways."

* * *

It was lunchtime, and they were serving hamburgers. I told them I was a vegetarian, and they made me a peanut butter and jelly sandwich. I hated jelly. I liked peanut butter and banana sandwiches. William sat down next to me.

"Why aren't you eating a hamburger?" he asked.

"Well, William, I'm a vegetarian," I replied.

"What's a vegetarian?"

"A vegetarian is a person who doesn't eat meat."

"Huh," he thought out loud. "Why don't you eat meat?"

"I find the killing of animals distasteful. I couldn't kill an animal, so why should I eat animals others have killed for me?" I said.

"Huh," he said again and took a beat. "Hey, can I have half of your sandwich?"

"Why? You have a whole hamburger there in front of you."

William looked up to me and smiled. "I'm a vegetarian now."

* * *

William spent the rest of the day showing me around. Not that there was much to see. There was a common room, the cafeteria, the smoking area outside, and our bedrooms. There were two to a room. I was scared of who I would be sharing a room with.

"You'll probably be in here with Matty. I think it's the only bed left."

"Who was in it before?" I asked.

"Charles. I don't want to tell you about Charles. It might scare you."

* * *

It was getting late, and it was time for pills. I hadn't seen a psychiatrist yet, so I was left alone. A tech walked me to my room. A fat balding man was laying on one of the two beds, the one closest to the window. He was sleeping peacefully. The room was dark, unnaturally so. I couldn't see a lamp or a light switch anywhere. I would later learn that the rooms were always dark to create a sedating effect. It was intentional. Intentional darkness was a *tactic*.

I lay in bed and realized that I hadn't seen a coincidence all day. Something about William grounded me. Took away my powers. Even so, I knew that I was gifted beyond all reason. I was only there because they didn't know what to do with me until the government arrived with scientists. I wondered if the scientists' tests would hurt.

20

Five Years, Divisionism and Anarchy, Red Scare

Naomi's funeral was rather unremarkable. Family, friends, coworkers, and the such. I went through the motions of a grieving boyfriend, and it wasn't too bad. It's not like the funeral service was very long, and I didn't have to speak. That was left up to her family. They had special vegetarian food for me at the repast. The food was absolutely amazing: cranberry brie bites, falafel with spicy mint tahini dip, black bean fritters — I could go on. If Naomi was there (well, *cancer* Naomi anyway), she would have gorged herself senseless.

I was now sitting at the funeral home waiting for a small urn of Naomi's remains. They split the remains up for loved ones these days, everyone getting a small urn. I thought it was rather considerate, although I wished that they had a delivery service. Who wants to sit in the lobby of a place like this? I thought I was done with depressing lobbies after Naomi had died. I had my journal with me.

> Most recently, she robbed a crematorium, armed with a GLOCK 45. Not realizing there was no cash on the premises, she opted for the ashes of a recently departed. In what could only be described as dumb luck, she was handed the remains of David Bowie. The obvious thing for her to do would be to freebase the ashes and ascend. But she chose not to. Instead, she bought a two-stage Pro Series II Vogel model rocket from Estes. No, she didn't load the ashes into the rocket before she launched it. Instead, as the rocket took off, she snorted David Bowie. She'd previously had a bad experience freebasing her beloved mother, Esther.

Daniel Radcliffe speaking of his ex-girlfriend to a class at the Met Film School, 2021

There was a Seurat print on the wall next to me and magazines on the coffee table. A part of me wanted to look through them for another magical journal, but I didn't. I mean how much magic could one person take? There was Russian folk music playing, and I thought it a little too festive for the setting.

> I believe that Neo-Impressionism was the birthplace of the avant-garde in painting. Chromoluminarism did away with the mixing palette. Painters, such as those in the Pointillism movement, believed that combining individualized dots of color achieved maximum luminosity. While this is scientifically

> implausible, we can see elements of that theory today in the modern television screen. But I digress. By not using a mixing palette, your work has a certain element of shittiness to it. It is a poor imitation of Signac, and it actually makes me physically sick. I might vomit all over it if I continue this examination. Truly, I think your work will give me diarrhea if I don't leave right this second. I love it. Load it into my van, quickly. It will look great in the guest bathroom next to my Seurat.

Robert Redford to Chuck Close, 1998

Vomiting, I thought. Would I miss the constant vomiting? Thinking about the vomiting, I became the saddest I had been since Naomi died. Yes, I thought. I would miss the vomiting.

> He called me over to his ham radio, visibly shaken, and said, "Honey, I found a secret numbers station. It's sending out a coded message to field operatives, and nobody knows where the originating signal is being broadcast from. It sounds Russian. Do these numbers mean anything to you?" There was an oddly synthesized voice repeating the numbers 36–24–34. "Well, that is my bust/waist/hip measurement," I said jokingly. He didn't laugh. Instead, he grabbed me by the shoulders and asked, "Are you now or have you ever been a member of the Communist Party of the United States?" I refused to answer the question. It was silly. I would not let McCarthyism define my body. Also, I had sworn an oath, and I wouldn't give an inch

> to the capitalist swine I called husband.

Geena Davis recounting the incident with her husband, Jeff Goldblum, to Susan Sarandon, 1988

The funeral director's assistant, a boy no older than sixteen, asked me to come to the counter. There was a little bronze urn, no larger than an egg, sitting there. Wow, they must have had to divide Naomi up into a lot of urns for it to be so tiny, I thought. She was extremely skinny though, so maybe her ashes were sparse.

"Here's Naomi," the boy said, gesturing to the egg of an urn.

"You mean 'here's *part* of Naomi,'" I said. I was sweating all of a sudden.

"I'm sorry sir, I'm not quite sure-" I cut him off. The room started to spin. My vision was blurry.

"And that can't be Naomi anyway. Naomi is always vomiting. It's so small, where is the vomit supposed to go?"

"Sir?"

I fainted right there in the Earl F. Bosworth Funeral Home.

21

Sydney, at the Institution

It wasn't until my second day, when I was a bit more acclimated, that I truly realized how deplorable the conditions there were. The techs would use cigarettes as bargaining chips, only allotting them if we did what they asked. They laughed at us when we went through episodes. During the day, if the meds made us sleepy, they would have us sleep on the piss-stained rugs so they didn't have to monitor the bedrooms. It was clear that the techs were the enemy.

I finally met with the psychiatrist, Dr. Singh. He was a soft-spoken Indian man in his seventies with deeply wrinkled skin. His wrinkles were his defining feature, cracks in reddish-brown clay. We were in a small unremarkable room, him at his desk and me on a chair seemingly made for children. He stared at my chart for about ten minutes. We sat in silence.

He broke the silence, saying that he was prescribing me seven medications. Lithium, risperidone, clonazepam, and four others I can't remember.

"Why so many pills?" I asked.

"Well, your brain isn't working right." That was his diagnosis? I expected medical terminology.

"That's it? My brain isn't working right?"

"Your thoughts are broken." he said, nonchalantly.

* * *

William introduced me to Sydney. Sydney was a woman in her forties who looked like she was in her sixties. She was skinnier than cancer Naomi. Tall and gaunt, her hair was four shades of brown and gray, frazzled like she was electrocuted in an old Charlie Chaplin movie. She could have been pretty in another life, I thought. She grabbed me by the arm and led me to the smoking area outside.

There was a manhole cover, which seemed odd as we weren't on a public street. She kept stomping on it with her right foot.

"That's my brother," she said.

"Your brother is down there?" I asked.

"No, this is my brother," she replied, stomping away. "Will you try?" Two techs, no older than twenty, were sitting close by and laughing at her.

"Sure, Sydney," I replied. I would try my hardest through this metaphysical soup we were now floating in, I thought. I stomped my right foot hard on the manhole cover. I stomped again, really trying to make something happen. I kept stomping.

William shouted, "Harder!" The techs were laughing so hard that they could barely catch their breath. I stomped harder. As hard as one could stomp. I alternated between my right and left feet.

"David?" she said, staring at me lovingly in my eyes. I stopped stomping. "David, is that you?" she asked me. Tears welled up in her eyes. Yes, she would have been beautiful in another life.

"Yes it's me," I said. It was a kindness I thought. Surely I was a better avatar than stomps on a manhole cover.

"I thought you died in the Everglades? With the airboat crash."

"No, Sydney. I'm here." She grabbed me and littered my face with kisses. She hugged me, and I could feel her ribs poking me. She squeezed so hard I thought one of her ribs would run me through. She was crying, and she looked a little faint. I brought her over to a bench and sat her down.

"David, you're back. I've missed you so much."

"Yes, I'm back. I'm alive," I said. The techs stopped laughing as they looked at her. As if she had been cured.

"I love you, David."

"I love you too, Sydney."

After that, everyone on the ward called me David. I now had two recruits. William and Sydney. They were loyal to me. To David.

22

Soroca District—Her Fashion Fits, Capillarity, Truth Serum, Riemannian Riff Raff, Windowpane,

I didn't think much about the fainting incident. It was a mourning episode, obviously. It was shock. Simple as that.

I was back at my apartment, and I turned on the television. There was a documentary on about phone sex workers in a dying industry due to the Internet. I turned it off, as it wasn't very interesting. I went over to my record collection and selected an Archers of Loaf record. I opened my journal.

> I'll move to Bădiceni, and you can move to Grigorăuca. We'll listen to Archers of Loaf when we meet on the weekends, and I'll scratch "She's an indie rocker, and nothing's gonna stop her," into your right ear. I'll move an inch to the bottom of the lobe, my nose now plugging the canal. My mouth is now parallel to your Adam's apple as it reverberates in a distorted

> coloratura. Now take your pants off.

Cyndi Lauper having phone sex with Alex Trebek shortly before his passing, 2020

> OK, I'm ready. You want me to take my pants off? OK, where should I put them? Got it. Rock hard? Not so much igneous or metamorphic. I'd say sedimentary. Yes, sedimentary. You want me to put what where? Got it. What is the method of locomotion? My choice, huh. Well, since you said that you made it wet, and it's approaching a narrow tube, I'll say capillary action. It moves against gravity using adhesion, cohesion, and surface tension. Yeah, that's it. Now what? Wait you want me to do what on your what? Excuse me, but that would require a foundation in evidence and repeated testing to have a predictive ability. How am I supposed to posit when... wait, I think its happening!

Bill Nye the Science Guy calling into a phone sex hotline, 1982

I opened Naomi's bedside drawer to see what drugs we had. Sure enough, there was acid, which is exactly what I was hoping to find. I needed one last outing with Naomi at Times Square. With the ghost of Naomi. I was sure she was a ghost by now. I put two tabs in a little baggie —one for me and one for her.

* * *

I opened my journal on the train ride into the city.

> Working on the set of Dirty Work was like being a test subject under the CIA's MKUltra project. Bob Saget was a great director and all, but he didn't do anything about Don Rickles dosing me with LSD. Even though Don only had one scene, that scene took days to film as we couldn't stop laughing at his quips. In one take, he did all of his jokes in Yiddish. Maybe he didn't dose me with LSD after all. Maybe I just couldn't bear the thought that nobody would ever be as funny as Don, not even Norm. Or maybe I just did too much ketamine and fell into a k-hole like I did about twenty minutes ago. Christ almighty, you have voluptuous breasts!

Artie Lange speaking to Queen Latifah, 2002

I was a bit unsure of my plan to take one last acid outing to Times Square with Naomi's ghost, but Don Rickles assured me it was a good plan.

> I took a class on Riemannian geometry before I was expelled from William Lyon Mackenzie Collegiate Institute. All was fine and dandy until I learned of the postulate that every pair of straight lines intersect. Maybe I misunderstood, but the notion that

> parallelism was a myth was too much for me to bear. Against my professor's advice, I took the weight of this concept to the multiverse theory. Our parallel timelines would eventually intersect; one day, Julie and I would kiss again in infinite ways. Oh, Julie. They thought I was high on LSD when I jumped off the roof of the dormitory, but I was really jumping for joy in a highly psychotic state. I only broke my ass bone, or whatever they call it. You know, the bone just above your ass.

Howie Mandel speaking of his lesser known college incident to Dave Chappelle at the premier of Half Baked, 1998

Howie Mandel agreed. It was definitely a good plan. Maybe I would get closure, although I wasn't quite sure what that meant. Was that one of the steps of grieving? Would it mean that Naomi would no longer exist to me?

> I regulate my own damn body, like the chambered nautilus. The growth of my soul as I age makes it necessary for it to travel to different parts of my body. When I was young, my soul resided in my sinuses. In the '60s, it meandered its way into my lungs. When I exhaled, parts of my soul, my Atman, joined the Brahman: the universal soul. Now, in my twilight years, what's left of it resides in my small bowel. So, as you insert your mechanical serpent into my anus, take heed, as you will be peering into the depth of my soul. Please lubricate thoroughly, and prepare for a

> wild ride into what's left of my very being.

Timothy Leary warning his doctor before the colonoscopy started, 1991

I had Timothy Leary's blessing. Now I knew that my trip to Times Square was a *mandate.*

23

David, at the Institution

I don't remember anything about my third day at the institution. I just know that something bad had happened to me.

24

The Violence of Georgia, Amery Ice Shelf, Sapphic Barflies, You Don't Have to put on the Red Light

On my way to Times Square, I decided to stop at a bar. I don't remember the name. I had just dropped the acid, so I had some time for it to kick in. I could read my journal a bit. The bartender, a lumberjack of a man with colorful tattooed sleeves asked me what I was having. I was feeling a bit adventurous.

"What is your favorite drink?" I asked.

"That would be a Cooperstown cocktail," he said. I had never heard of it. Exactly what I was looking for.

"Well then, one Cooperstown cocktail for me."

I took the journal out of my messenger bag.

> I sat at the sticky bar, sipping on a Cooperstown cocktail. It's wrong to say that gin makes a man mean, as being mean is a precursor in the metabolic pathway

of our very being. I found a scribbled poem on a napkin.

His hunter's blood
Bloodies the hunter's
Bolt action bravado
As he primps
And preens
In blue-collar jeans
Someone show her
The way out of
Georgia

I was feeling tipsy, whimsical and geographical, so I flipped the napkin over, and I wrote a poem of my own, trying to capture the original's style.

Your bloodshot heart
And shot put eyes
Push clots
Through a main lined
Railway from
Nebraska
To wherever
You hang
These days
Maybe an
Ohio
River boat
I'm drowning
Deeply behind

> *Avast!*
>
> On sober days, I often wonder if she ever made it out. Maybe to Nebraska or Ohio, where men are still mean, but not as mean as in Georgia.

The opening from Crispin Glover's unpublished memoir, tentatively titled "Gin and Juice"

I used to write poems for Naomi, years before the cancer. They weren't very good. Certainly not as good as the poems from *Uzis and Lean and all of the Wars in Between.* I wondered why I had stopped. Maybe it's just one of those things, when you get familiar with someone, that you stop doing. They should have a taxonomy for the different stages of relationships. A taxonomy that describes things you start and stop doing during highly defined periods of time with a lover. Like when do you stop calling them a *lover* and start calling them a *girlfriend*? And when do you switch from *girlfriend* to *partner*? I like things to be named and categorized. I sipped on my Cooperstown cocktail. It was rather good.

> He was working at the United States Advisory Committee on Antarctic Names, US-ACAN, when his appendix burst. Four hours later, the morphine changed his idea of taxonomy. All of the sudden the naming of things became erotic. This condition persisted throughout his career, and he had to hide erections constantly. He became aroused when he named his Alaskan Malamute after the band Blondie. I

> believe this is why he never had children. How could he ever name them?

Sandra Cisneros discussing her cousin with Downtown Julie Brown on a flight to Antwerp, 1985.

There were two lesbians at the bar, clearly in love. I wondered what stage of relationship they were in. I would say they were transitioning from *lovers* to *girlfriends*. The taxonomy needed to name transitional stages as well.

> She spun me all around, the conflicting states of my motion and sight turning me into a cosmonaut of sickness. It was the Coriolis illusion making me nauseated, not the unexpected cellulite or spider veins. Not her bloated tummy. I hadn't seen her in more than three decades, and I wondered what mechanism would make the bile rise if I wasn't twirling in the tulips. Would the sick still travel up my throat? Would I still vomit on her yellow summer dress? I cried a child's cry when she told me it was her favorite dress. I suddenly loved her again like I did when we were sixteen and pretty. Please take the bourbon away from me. I've drunk too much, and I'm feeling nauseated. I don't want to fall in love with you too. You're too dumb and skinny.

Sarah Paulson speaking to Cara Delevingne at the Cubbyhole, as overheard by Rosie O'Donnell, NYC, 2023

The acid was starting to kick in. I had some time though before my plan to peak at Times Square with the ghost of Naomi. Pat Benatar was playing in the background. It reminded me of an eighties party Naomi and I had gone to before the cancer. She dressed as Madonna (God she looked good), and I put a box around my head in a meager attempt to be Max Headroom.

> I am the principle of homonymy. You can classify me in any way you choose. But If I am the first named boy, you can never name another as me. It's almost biblical, I confess. But my bible is the International Code of Zoological Nomenclature. A code that cannot be broken, even by a sexy woman like you. So name me, baby. "Hit me with your best shot," like Pat Benatar would say. I adore her. But let's keep on track. If you are to name me, make it singular. Stand before me naked or clothed. It's all the same to this singular soul. Taxonomy turns me on more than your fishnet stockings or bare calves. But if you dress up like Pat Benatar on the cover of "Get Nervous," straight jacket and all, you can call me anything you want. Bob, even.

Sting speaking to a lost prostitute he picked up on Trafalgar Square, London, 1984

* * *

I was a few blocks away from Times Square when the acid really started to kick in, but I was OK enough to make it. I had a lot of experience with LSD. As my thoughts trailed to my first time dropping acid, someone tapped me on the shoulder from behind. It was Naomi. *Before the cancer* Naomi. I had forgotten how beautiful she was before her suffering. I took out my little baggie and pressed the second tab to her tongue with my index finger.

"Are you ready, my love?" I asked. "We're about four months overdue."

"I've really missed this." she said. I didn't know if she meant our little acid retreats or life in general. Or maybe being with me. Maybe she missed being with me.

"Me too," I said.

A tear dropped from my eye. We walked hand in hand to Times Square.

25

Latonya, at the Institution

In the morning, it was time for pills. We gauged our time by pills and cigarettes. Pills first thing in the morning, cigarettes every hour (unless we were being punished), and pills before lights out. A particularly cruel tech came over to me with a tiny paper cup of eight pills. I counted them. I was only supposed to have seven. The eighth one stood out, as it was all black. I had never seen a black pill before. It was a capsule.

"There's an extra pill here," I said.

"Just take the meds, and don't give me a hard time," he said.

"Check my chart. I'm only supposed to have seven pills. Go ask Dr. Singh if you have to."

"Look, I'm too busy for this shit. Take the fucking meds."

"What's your name?" I asked.

"Jimmy. Why, are you going to report me?" he laughed.

I glanced at William and Sydney to my left. They wouldn't leave my side.

"Jimmy." I said to them.

William scratched something down in his Jesus poetry book.

I took the pills but palmed the black one.

* * *

We were sitting on a couch that smelled like piss. I hadn't seen a tech clean anything since I had been there. They just lounged around or played on their phones. William was keeping track of their schedules.

There was a Black girl, no older than eighteen, rocking back and forth and talking to the wall next to us. She could have been a model. All legs, a perfectly rounded face, and a long neck.

"Who's that?" I asked William.

"That's Latonya. She's schizophrenal."

"You mean schizophrenic." William jotted that down in his Jesus notebook.

"She's talking to her girlfriend. That's all she does." Sydney said.

"And she's always smiling," William added.

I stood up and went over to Latonya.

"Hey, Latonya. I'm David." I liked my new name. It was surely biblical. Latonya smiled a perfect smile and continued to rock back and forth, talking to the wall. Not quite talking, really, but rather mouthing words with the tiniest of vocalizations sneaking out every now and then.

My delusions of grandeur started creeping out again that day. I wondered how long it would take for the scientists to come get me. There was a lot to study. I was a beacon for synchronicity, and I could bend it at will. There must be all sorts of military applications for that sort of thing, I thought. I had told William to keep an eye out for men in lab coats.

I took the black pill from out of my pocket. It was a sign. I asked Latonya to open her mouth. I placed it on her tongue like a communion wafer.

She swallowed the pill and smiled again at me. She went back to talking to the wall. To her girlfriend.

We waited for about an hour for the pill to do something. Sydney was impatient, but loyal. She stayed seated. Out of nowhere, Latonya sat down on the floor, cross legged against the wall. She started to cry. She cried for a good half an hour. When she stopped, I sat down next to her.

"David?" she uttered, her voice now hoarse, talking at a normal volume as if for the first time.

"Yes, Latonya?"

"Where did she go? Where did Jess go?"

"She had to leave for a bit," I said.

"OK," she replied, "What am I supposed to do now?"

"Go talk to William. He'll fill you in."

* * *

By now, the techs were starting to catch on. William, Sydney, and Latonya marched behind me wherever I went. Sydney stood guard while I used the bathroom. Latonya would break off now and then and whisper to other patients.

"Go see David," she would say.

Every time I walked by a tech, they looked a little spooked. Like I was a magical healer. They tried to keep me segregated from the other patients, but the institution was too small and understaffed.

By my fourth day at the institution, I had healed about ten patients in all. Enough for a small platoon.

26

Sweet Circumstellar Disks, Andromeda Antics, The Semiconductor Industry, Sunday Morning Brings the Dawn In

There are ten 50-foot long granite benches in Times Square, and Naomi and I would always take our time selecting the perfect spot. It had to be crowded, but not too crowded. Just the right amount of crowded that allowed us to feel like part of the scenery. Like anonymous characters in a stock photo.

It had gotten dark out, and Times Square was flashing like capitalist fireworks. Lights and digital signs advertising everything everywhere. Tourists gawking like they were in a Ridley Scott science fiction movie.

"I have to show you something," I said. I pulled out my journal camouflaged as Julio Cortázar's *Hopscotch.*

"Oh. I don't like that book," Naomi said, slightly frowning.

I smirked and said, "I know, my love. This isn't that. This is something magical. This is called *Strung Out on Plenitudes*. First, before I show you, I want you to look up at the sky. I want you to imagine that we can see actual stars through all of the lights. Pretend that we're astronauts."

"OK," Naomi giggled. Her trip was starting. She always giggled at the beginning of her trips.

"Now come back to Earth."

"So we're not astronauts anymore?" she asked.

"No. Now we are thaumaturges. Magicians. I opened the journal and read out loud.

> You are like a chemically peculiar star. I can estimate your distance by your annual parallax shift. 142 light years away from me, you are young, just 10 million years old. You hang out with the sailor boys in the Beta Pictoris moving group, keeping me jealous and unnerved. Your infrared excess has all the sailor boys swooning, and I'm like the comic book Infinaut, preening for your attention, lost between galaxies, and aching for your solar flares.

Neil deGrasse Tyson to one of his unnamed fans, during the allegations, 2018

"See," I said, "This journal alludes to our immediate past in a wave of synchronicity. They are performative pop culture stories, quotes, and secrets with encoded messages, telling us where we just were. What we just saw. What we were just thinking about. But that's not all." I turned the page and continued to read.

> OK, so check it. The opening scene shows the interior living quarters of an outer space mining vessel. Our main character, a lowly space merchant named Gregory Samsarian, wakes up transformed into an alien insectoid creature. The rest of the crew is terrified and locks him in a containment bay. Unable to negotiate trade arrangements with nearby planetary federations, Gregory is soon neglected, while the rest of the crew runs out of resour- wait, let me finish. What do you mean by Kafkaesque? I've never heard of the term. Is it German? I've already got Julia Roberts lined up to play Gregory's sister, Greteria.

Spike Jonze's elevator pitch to A24 for his script titled The Andromeda Metamorphosis, 2021

Now look down. What do you see?

"A cockroach," she giggled.

"Yes, *Kafka's cockroach.* In *outer space.* Do you see now? This book also alludes to our immediate future in the same type of synchronicity."

"Wow, you're really tripping," she said.

"No, this is real. Let's play the game we always play when we come here."

"The one where we pick out a person and guess who they are?"

"Yes," I said. "You pick."

Naomi paused, squinted her eyes, and pointed to a tall well-groomed man in a fitted suit carrying a brief case.

"He's a CEO from downtown who works in the semiconductor industry," she said.

"Now check this out," I said, turning the page.

> This business? I am this business. I am the supra-entity that excretes innovation. There is no need for an Entity Relationship Diagram to show my supra-attributes and supra-relationships. In fact, I am the Übermensch. The goddamn Superman of semiconductors. I bleed into solar cells. I urinate into supercomputers. I ejaculate into automobiles. I goddamn flatulate into the very smartphones that you glue your smug faces to. Fire me? Who will save Metropolis? Larry in accounting?

Michael R. Hsing, CEO of Monolithic Power Systems to the Board of Directors, 2024

"Wow." Her eyes were glowing now. She smiled a ghost smile. Looking all around her, she pointed and said, "That lady over there. She writes about Buddhism."

I smiled at her enthusiasm. The cheer in her voice. Like she had never heard the word *leukemia* before. Like she had never vomited once in her entire life.

> On that Sunday morning, she decided she would live the life of a bodhisattva. She would strive towards enlightenment. Her bodhicitta, her spontaneous wish to attain bodhi, happened when she was watching an episode of Tidying Up with Marie Kondo. She would only keep possessions that would "spark joy." She

> categorized all of her belongings, and she found only one that sparked joy. She noticed its battery was dead and replaced it, lovingly. Inspired, she would soon write a book on tantric masturbation, which I never read, as I chose to forgo my personal nirvana.

John Lithgow describing the seminal Sunday morning with his anonymous friend to Vanilla Ice on the sands of South Beach, Miami, 2023

"This is amazing. And you promise it's not just the drugs?" she asked.

"Cross my heart and hope to —"

We both fell silent. I started to sob uncontrollably.

27

Dr. Singh, at the Institution

On my fifth day at the institution, I was scheduled to meet with Dr. Singh again for a progress report. This time, there were two fat middle-aged women in the room with us. They could have been twins. It seemed odd that they were there.

"So how are you doing?" Dr. Singh asked.

"I'm fine. I've always been fine. I shouldn't be here."

"Why do you think you are here?"

"Well, you said my thoughts were broken," I replied.

"Ah yes, I did, didn't I?" His age and accent made him talk slowly. He opened my chart, and the four of us sat in silence for a good five minutes. He was an ancient scholar reading forbidden texts.

"Do you think your thoughts are broken?" he asked.

The two ladies looked at each other in shock at the paradox. They were listening to Epicurus teaching his philosophy.

"Do I think my thoughts are broken? How does that even work?"

Dr. Singh laughed and said, "I see what you mean there. You

are very astute, young man."

Was this some kind of game? Would I need to decode a cipher? He paused again, reading over my chart.

"Tell me about the scientists."

"What do you want to know? They are scientists. They study things. Come up with hypotheses. That kind of stuff," I said.

"And who do they work for?"

"The government," I said. "Specifically for DARPA."

"And why do they have an interest in you?" he asked. The fat woman to my left sneezed.

"Because of my powers. I can see synchroncities in everything and bend them to my will."

"Yes, surely that could have military applications," he said.

"Exactly!"

"Ms. Torres?" He looked over to the woman at my right.

"Oh yes, um. I'm Ms. Torres, the Facilities Director. And this is Mrs. Altridge, a social worker here. We wanted to talk to you about something." she said.

"I'm sick of all of this talking. When do I get to go home?"

"I assure you that Dr. Singh is working on that. Right Dr. Singh?" He held a pen up to his cracked lips, smiling and shaking his head up and down in a slow bob.

"I have something to show you," Ms. Torres said. She pulled out a notebook. It was William's notebook.

"That's William's," I said.

"Yes, it is." She opened it up carefully like it was an old tomb. All I could see was red scribbles. She turned the page. More red scribbles. She turned about five more pages, and all of them were just red scribbles with some purple coming out where the blue words had been before the defacement.

"All of his poetry. It's gone," I said. My eyes started to well up.

"Do you know who did this?" Mrs. Altridge asked, speaking up for the first time. She was curt.

"No."

"Well, one of our techs found this under your mattress." She brandished a red crayon like a dagger.

"That's not mine," I pleaded, tears streaming down my face. "I help these people! I cure them!" I shouted. The fat women flinched away. Dr. Singh pressed some type of button hidden somewhere, and two techs and a nurse rushed into the room.

"Two milligrams of Haldol," Dr. Singh shouted over the commotion. The techs were restraining me, and the nurse already had the syringe at the ready. They must have drilled this scenario a million times.

As I started to doze off, the last thing I saw was Jimmy the tech's face, smiling.

"Got you, motherfucker."

* * *

I woke up in my bedroom, and William and Latonya were hovering above me. I noticed Sydney and two other converts guarding the door.

"William, it wasn't me," I said.

"I know who it was. What are we going to do?"

Latonya said, "We need a plan."

"Before the scientists come to get you," William said. "It has to be before the scientists come to get you."

28

Gravity's Nose Bleed, The Theory of Forms, Jain Dharma, Carabidae, Full Contact Folly, No Body—No Grave

"Why didn't you tell me about this journal when, well, when..."

"When you were alive?"

"Yeah," she said.

"I didn't want to worry you. At first I thought I was having another episode like in 2017. I found a journal about that too. An autobiography that I didn't write."

"I don't get it."

"Neither do I," I sighed. A little while passed and we both sat in silence. My trip was peaking, and Times Square was melting upwards. I was about to speak, but she went first.

"Why did you never ask me to marry you?"

"I'm not sure. I meant to. I mean..."

"The cancer?"

"I'm not sure," I said. What a stupid and cowardly thing to say. I didn't think it was the cancer. Or uncertainty. Or any other damn reason. I guess it was just something I never got around to doing.

"Read more to me," she said.

> Normally, when you're punched in the nose, lights go dim, and you get an aerial view of Mare Imbrium, like the lunar cataclysm that created the massive crater itself. You are pushed out of yourself and into a dimension of numb residue. You quietly censure yourself in milliseconds before you come to. Now, like in this case, being knocked out is an entirely different equation. Your brain has time to unconsciously consider all of the possibilities. Should you have brought a switchblade? Should you have brought a tire iron? Should you have called the police? Should you have talked it out? Should you have brought a wedding ring?

Thomas Pynchon describing to his son, Jackson, the night he proposed to his wife, Melanie Jackson, after she punched him in the nose, 2002

We sat in silence after that for what seemed like hours.

"Read another to me."

"OK, but we have to watch what we think. The journal will just throw it right back in our faces."

> I'm a firm believer in Platonic realism. Think up a new idea, and it will exist forever as literal reality. Literal reality. What I mean is that if it's valid and holds it all

> together, then it'll become part of the universe. And excuse my French, but your motherfucking knees, gall bladder, and tongue don't matter in these parts. It's metaphysical. I don't need a gun. I won't slip you a note. Keep your wits, empty the till, and watch what you think.

Squizzy Taylor's threat as he robbed the Bendigo & Adelaide Bank, 1928

We both laughed at how meta it was. Everything seemed to be meta these days. They were always writing movies about movies and books about books.

"Keep going. I don't want this to end," she said. A beetle landed in her hair, and I brushed it off gently.

"You always were gentle with life," she said. "Like a Jain."

> He drank Pabst Blue Ribbon from the cranial fossa of a skull. As if a warlock. A breaker of oaths. A deceiver. He was raised on Dinosaur Jr. and Kool 100s in a mystical kind of way. "Every girl's a suspect, and every boy's your friend," as J would sing, creating a formative distrust of his lovers and of himself. He studied Jainism, although did not practice it under the gaslights of 2:00 AM fistfights. One night he got punched in the nose, and it changed everything. Jain Dharma was now present in every action. He even went barefoot to avoid the killing of insects. The only exception to this nonviolence would be the slaughter of fruit flies, as he held his papayas sacred. More sacred

> than reaching siddha and moksha. More sacred than the inside of my thighs.

Angelina Jolie talking to Billy Bob Thornton about her first boyfriend as overheard by Spike Lee on a private jet headed to France, 2002

The beetle came back for more, as if taunting my forgiveness.

> She was named Nebria Haida after the beetle. The beetle on the back, under the shirt, giving gnashing tickles, and sickeningly symmetrical. We didn't care much for her presence. She sat under a tree not so much Bodhi as apple, far away from the rest of the parents. Sarah said it was a "hot girl summer" so I joined Nebria because, you know what, I can't do this shit anymore.

MC Hammer whispering to the ghost of Gallus Jakob Alt after taking a hero dose of mescaline, 2023

We sat for a while, and I held her. No games. No journal. No Times Square. Maybe I was in her dimension now? Everything was quiet, and the lights dimmed. Was this what it felt like to be a ghost?

"Is that a sumo wrestler? In Times Square?" Naomi asked. I was startled back into reality, looking straight at a sumo wrestler, a humongous boulder rolling down the street.

"Well look at that. That certainly is a sumo wrestler, my love. Want to see what the journal has to say about it?"

"Obviously."

> Fujinishiki Akira, the sumo wrestler, was all set to appear on The Tonight Show Starring Johnny Carson on July 14th, 1964 after winning the top makuuchi division tournament championship. He was known for his strong tachi-ai, and when asked to perform this powerful charge backstage for Johnny, there was a problem in translation. He directed his tachi-ai right at Johnny, knocking him into the craft service table. Johnny stood up, covered in condiments, and peeled a piece of lunch meat from his face. He handed it to Fujinishiki, saying "I always knew you all were full of baloney. And that's why Nagasaki had to happen." The drummer on set heard the quip and played a timid rimshot.

Henry Morgan, explaining to Dan Aykroyd how he replaced Fujinishiki Akira at the last minute as a guest on The Tonight Show, 1977.

"Was I cremated like I wanted to be? Or did my parents insist on a burial?"

"You were cremated. I have a little urn of you. As big as an egg." I motioned an oval shape with my fingers. I was starting to feel sober. A deep wave of sadness encompassed me.

"One more?" I asked.

"One more," she said and kissed me with ghost lips on the forehead.

> There was no body to be found, so we erected a plain cenotaph monument on which was inscribed:
>
> *Here lies nobody*
> *Literally no body*
> *So we are reduced to physicalism*
> *No mind–body dualism*
> *Can be had here*
> *Anymore*
> *Forevermore*
>
> We did not list her name or period of life, for now we bathed in monism. Without the body there is no spacetime or taxonomy. No need for an empty grave. After all, she could just be missing forever, and with an empty grave one could make a stupid Schrödinger joke. Our poor cat, Lenola, did not like tomfoolery. She liked tummy rubs and dragging her ass across the carpet.

From the prologue to Carl Sagan's unpublished autobiography

And just like that, Naomi was gone. I sat on the bench until sunrise, thinking about nothing in particular.

29

Mutiny - at the Institution

Sydney was the distraction. It was an extremely simple plan. It was at the beginning of the nightly pill ritual, when the techs had little paper pill cups all lined up on an aluminum tray. One by one they would deliver the appropriate meds to each patient. William had stolen a lighter from one of the techs who lit our cigarettes for us. During the planning stage, we gave that tech the code name "Matchsticks." Standing up on a table, Sydney lit a box of tissues on fire. There were tissues boxes everywhere at the institution, but they were rarely used. Surprisingly, nobody really cried here all that much. I think the meds controlled that.

All six of the techs stopped prepping for pill time and rushed over to Sydney and her fire. William was my armory officer. He had gathered scissors, sharpened pencils, and he had even fashioned a few shanks out of tooth brushes. William was special, so the techs underestimated him. One by one, he distributed the weapons to the ten others of my flock. The healed ones. My infantry. Latonya, our communications officer, had briefed them all on the plan prior. They all surrounded the commotion that was Sydney, her box of fire, and the techs. One of the techs smacked the fire out with his sweater, and another two restrained Sydney.

"Get your hands off of her!" Latonya yelled. She had barely been able to whisper when I first met her.

William and his army closed in on the techs. Jimmy tried to grab one of the infantry, and William jumped on his back, a pair of scissors at his throat. The techs all froze. Latonya ordered them all to sit on the piss-stained carpet, backs against the wall. Her voice was now commanding. They complied, outnumbered two-to-one.

A silence overcame the ward. Sydney, Latonya, and William went to the doors and barricaded them with chairs seemingly made for children.

In the planning stage, we had considered our mission, and it wasn't violence or escape. It was healing. That's why we started the operation right before it was pill time. Sydney went over to the pill tray and selected six paper cups like she was playing roulette. William grabbed six bottles of water.

One by one, Sydney gave a pill cup and a bottle of water to each of the techs.

"Swallow the pills," William ordered. At first they were hesitant, but William brandished his scissors at Jimmy's throat again.

So they swallowed the pills, and we all just stood there, waiting for them to be healed. After about thirty minutes, Jimmy started having a seizure. He died shortly there afterwards.

* * *

Months later, during the investigation, I tried to take responsibility for Jimmy's death. It didn't matter though. They wound up sweeping the whole thing under the rug when it came out that Jimmy had been raping William for at least three months on a regular basis.

* * *

I was to be discharged the next day. They had no legal reason to keep me, as Dr. Singh determined I wasn't a threat to myself or others. They had no idea that I had orchestrated the mutiny. After all, I had just sat there and watched while my soldiers carried out the entire operation. Obviously, none of them had given me up.

Sydney, Latonya, and William were transferred to other places. I imagined it wasn't too pleasant for them.

Naomi came to pick me up.

"How are you, sweetheart?" she asked. We had been together about a year by then.

"I did something terrible."

"Hush. I'm sure it wasn't that bad. You can tell me about it after we get home. I made you vegetarian meatloaf," she said.

"You know what the worst part was?" Her eyes started to tear up in anticipation.

"What?" she asked.

"The scientists never came. Maybe my thoughts really are broken. I think I need help."

30

A Nearly Cosmopolitan Distribution, Sid and Nancy - Part 2, The Chimpanzee Genome Project, 8-bar Break: Mr. Mixx Cuts

A few days after Times Square, I was sitting on the couch. It felt like I as always sitting on the couch these days. I hadn't read *Strung Out on Plenitudes* since Times Square, and I turned off the Jacques Cousteau documentary I was watching. I opened it up my journal for what would be the last time.

> There are 67 known species of Escharella, starting alphabetically with Escharella abyssicola and ending with Escharella watersi. These Bryozoa, or what some plebeians would call "moss animals," have beautiful crowns of tentacles known as lophophores through which they eat. They are majestic oceanographers. And you know what? Not one of the 67 royal species

> of Escharella have their own Wikipedia page. Not even my favorite, Escharella capitata. This cannot stand. Someone get me the head of Wikipedia on the phone posthaste! The son of a bitch is going to learn a thing or two about how to properly manage an Internet!

Jean-Michel Cousteau at the age of 87, son of the famous Jacques Cousteau, screaming at his assistants as overheard by James Cameron, 2025

I let myself laugh. I had been rather somber since Times Square. Somber and lighter. I was a blue balloon soaring in the skies of Hoboken. I went to the kitchen to get a snack. Opening the cupboard, I looked down at Naomi's basket of pills. I noticed the Adderall. With all of the cancer medication, I forgot she had ADHD. I popped two, put the pill bottle in my pocket, and smirked. Maybe I *was* a drug addict after all. I loved amphetamines, and I could definitely use a pick-me-up. I grabbed a bag of Frito-Lay chips, and I sat back down on the couch.

> Methamphetamine is my true love, and you are just a groupie. You say you are a pining butterfly, but you are really just a lust-inducing firefly. I'm snorting the powder off of this here blade, while you wile me with damaged breasts and chapped lips. Don't tempt my knife, for beasts are meant for slaughter, and you, darling, are a cow with too many udders for such a delicate frame.

Sid Vicious to Nancy Spungen, minutes before he killed her at the Hotel Chelsea with his Jaguar Wilderness K-11 knife, October 12, 1978

I thought about when I had read the first Sid and Nancy story at the drugstore. My mind naturally drifted to the pregnancy test. We could have had a child, I thought, looking around at our cramped and messy apartment. We would have had to have gotten rid of a lot of stuff for the baby and lived a more ascetic lifestyle.

> Let's fuck in the Achaleshwar Mahadev Temple with the energy of Shakti. Let Lord Shiva record with his Panasonic AG-HPX300 and sell copies for 426 rupees. The Destroyer of worlds and purveyor of pop culture pornography. The funds will support our newly ascetic lifestyles.

Jane Goodall to her anonymous lover, as overheard by Dr. Dre on a bus to Sirohi

I had only one more quote left. There was no epilogue. Just then, someone knocked on the door.

"Hey there!" I said to my crippled friend. "Come in, let me grab you a glass of O.J."

He sat down on the La-Z-Boy.

"I came by to return this to you," he said, handing me *My Time at the Institution: An Autobiography* as I handed him his O.J.

"Oh, that." I had almost forgotten about it. "Did you read it?"

"Yes. I understand why you are a very sad man now."

"You know, I don't feel so sad today. You hungry?"

"Sure." he said.

"Let's go to a diner and grab some lunch."

He downed his glass of O.J. in one gulp and headed out the door. Before I followed him, I grabbed *Strung Out on Plenitudes* and read the last quote.

> We were riding four deep in the '78 Ford LTD. It was a custom job with added tail fins, porthole back windows, and purple and blue ghost flames. We rolled up to the toll booth on the turnpike, and I handed the operator a dollar. He stood there motionless and stared me dead in the eyes. I asked the old man what his problem was, and he replied, "Problems are for pussies, and the only pussy I see here is you." Before it could pop off, a Frito-Lay truck rear-ended us. Fresh Kid Ice yelled out from the back seat, "Head, booty, cock!" The toll booth operator smiled, did a little dance, and that's when I knew we had a hit single on our hands.

Uncle Luke of 2 Live Crew discussing the success of the song "H-B-C (Head, Booty & Cock)" on an unaired episode of the show "Between Two Ferns with Zach Galifianakis," 2008

I walked downstairs and a '78 Ford LTD with added tail fins, porthole back windows, and purple and blue ghost flames and all was parked outside my apartment building.

"This must be yours," I said.

"Yes. I'll drive."

"Ok, just watch out for any Frito-Lay trucks," I laughed.

He looked at me quizzically. I stopped him before he got in the car.

"Hey, I never did get your name."

"William. Like the young man in your journal," he said. "What's yours?"

"William, huh? Well in that case, I'd like it if you'd call me David."

www.ingramcontent.com/pod-product-compliance
Lightning Source LLC
Chambersburg PA
CBHW031347060726
47590CB00007B/2668